The Galaxy Needs You

WRITTEN BY

Caitlin Kennedy

ILLUSTRATED BY

Eda Kaban

DISNEP

LUCASFILM

P R E S S

LOS ANGELES
NEW YORK

© & TM 2019 Lucasfilm Ltd.

All rights reserved. Published by Disney · Lucasfilm Press, an imprint of Disney Book Group.

No part of this book may be reproduced or transmitted in any form or by any means,

electronic or mechanical, including photocopying, recording, or by any information storage

and retrieval system, without written permission from the publisher. For information address

Disney · Lucasfilm Press, 1200 Grand Central Avenue, Glendale, California 91201.

Printed in the United States of America

First Edition, December 2019

10 9 8 7 6 5 4 3 2 1

Library of Congress Control Number on file

FAC-034274-19312

ISBN 978-1-368-05182-8

Visit the official *Star Wars* website at: www.starwars.com.

Designed by Scott Piehl

H
ave you ever stopped to think
about how there is nobody else
in the galaxy who is exactly like you?

Nobody else has your hair . . .

or your eyes . . .

or your smile.

Nobody else is smart in the way

you're smart . . .

. . . or curious in the way
you're curious.

Nobody else likes the exact same

things you like . . .

. . . or is kind in the particular way
you're kind.

Nobody else is strong in the same way **you're strong . . .**

. . . or makes friends the way you do.

And nobody is brave the way
you're brave.

You are truly one of a kind.

You have everything inside yourself
that you need to succeed.

All you have to do is reach for it . . .

. . . and not be afraid.

No matter where the journey
takes you . . .

. . . or who you meet . . .

. . . or what you learn along

the way . . .

. . . know that it's okay to
make mistakes . . .

. . . as long as you face your problems
head-on . . .

. . . and fight for what you believe in.

Even if someone tries to tell you that you're nothing . . .

or nobody . . .

You can do hard things.

And you can fix things that
seem impossible to fix.

So hold on to what makes

you special . . .

. . . remember to look to the light . . .

. . . because the galaxy needs you . . .

And when things seem dark . . .

Stick with the friends who cheer you
on each step of the way.

. . . and work hard to learn and grow
every day.

. . . because there's nobody else like

you.